The Boxcar Children® Mysteries

THE MYSTERY OF THE LAKE MONSTER

created by
GERTRUDE CHANDLER WARNER

Illustrated by Charles Tang

ALBERT WHITMAN & Company
Morton Grove, Illinois

Library of Congress Cataloging-in-Publication Data

Warner, Gertrude Chandler, 1890–
The mystery of the lake monster/created by Gertrude Chandler Warner;
illustrated by Charles Tang.
p. cm —(The Boxcar children mysteries)
Summary: While visiting Lake Lucille in the Adirondack Mountains,
the Aldens hear stories about a monster in the lake and then encounter
evidence that it may be real.
ISBN 0-8075-5441-3 (hardcover)
ISBN 0-8075-5442-1 (paperback)
[1. Monsters–Fiction. 2. Lakes–Fiction.
3. Adirondack Mountains (N.Y.)–Fiction.
4. Brothers and sisters–Fiction. 5. Orphans–Fiction.
6. Mystery and detective stories.]
I. Tang, Charles, ill. II. Title.
III. Series: Warner, Gertrude Chandler, 1890–
Boxcar children mysteries.
PZ7.W244Mxf 1998   97-40301
[Fic]–dc21   CIP
                                AC

Cover art by David Cunningham.

Contents

CHAPTER 1

Into the Wilderness

Benny Alden leaned forward to stare out the window. "Wow," he said. "Look how tall all those mountains are!"

His brother, Henry, laughed. "Mountains are supposed to be tall, Benny. That's why they're called mountains."

"How tall *are* these mountains?" Benny asked.

Violet Alden looked up from the book she was reading. "It says here that the tallest mountain in the Adirondacks is Mt. Marcy. It's over five thousand feet tall."

"How tall am I?" asked Benny. He was six years old.

"Not over four feet tall," said Jessie Alden.

"I guess that these mountains are a *lot* taller than I am," said Benny.

Everybody in the car laughed.

The Aldens were on their way to spend a week at Lucille Lodge on Lake Lucille, high in the Adirondack Mountains in New York State.

"Are we almost there, Grandfather?" asked Jessie.

"Almost," he answered. Grandfather Alden slowed down and turned the car off the paved road onto a dirt road. The car bounced and bumped over the deep ruts. Tree branches clawed the windows.

The road twisted and turned, higher and higher. Benny could no longer see the tops of the mountains through the trees. At last Grandfather stopped in front of a huge wooden gate. On the gate, a carved sign said LUCILLE LODGE.

"I'll open the gate," said Jessie.

"I'll help," said Henry.

They jumped out of the car and opened the gate. After Grandfather Alden had driven through, they closed it again and hurried to get back into the car.

They followed the rough track through the trees, but still they didn't see Lake Lucille or Lucille Lodge.

"We're not lost, are we?" asked Violet.

"No," said Grandfather. "Look." He turned one more corner and the four Alden children gasped.

They were in a broad clearing. Ahead of them was a small, clear, beautiful lake, as blue as the sky it reflected. Steep walls of rock and wooded mountainside rose above it on every side. At the far end of the clearing right on the edge of the lake was an enormous two-story building made of wood. Wide porches with birch-branch railings ran around the building on the lower floor.

Grandfather drove forward and parked to one side of the building. As the Aldens got out of the car, a small, wiry woman with short dark hair and friendly green eyes came out of the building and walked toward them. "Welcome to Lucille Lodge," she said. "I'm Nora Parker. Everyone calls me Nora."

"James Alden," said Grandfather Alden. "And these are my grandchildren: Henry, Jessie, Violet, and Benny."

"And Watch," said Benny, patting his dog on the head.

"Hi," said Nora. She looked at Benny. "How old are you, Benny?"

"I'm six. Henry is fourteen, Jessie is twelve, Violet is ten." He paused and added, "I don't know how old Grandfather is."

"That's okay," said Nora, her smile widening.

"Or Watch, either," said Benny. "We found him when we were living in the box-car."

Seeing Nora's surprised look, the Alden children quickly explained how, when they had become orphans, they had gone to live in an old boxcar in the woods. They didn't know their grandfather was looking for

them. But he was, and when he found them, he brought them all to live with him in his big old house in Greenfield. To surprise them, and to make them feel more at home, he'd brought the boxcar home and put it behind the house so they could visit it whenever they wanted.

"That's some story," said Nora when they had finished. "But I'm glad to know you've lived in a boxcar. You might not find our cabins so very different!"

A man came out onto the porch and stood on the top step. He wasn't much taller than Nora. He had short brown hair and blue eyes. He was holding a large rolling pin in one hand. He raised the rolling pin. "That's the truth! You'll see," he said in a grim voice.

"Oh!" exclaimed Violet, her eyes widening when she saw the rolling pin.

The man looked at the raised rolling pin. He grimaced. "Sorry," he said.

Nora said, "This is Drew, my husband. He's the chef at the lodge."

The Aldens said hello. Drew nodded

curtly. "Welcome to mountain life," he said. "Mountain life about a hundred years ago, that is." With that he turned and walked back into the lodge.

Nora looked momentarily embarrassed. She cleared her throat and said, "Drew isn't used to living up here yet. But when he does get used to it, I know he'll love it as much as I do. Now let me take you to your cabin."

The Aldens got their suitcases and backpacks and followed Nora across the clearing to a trail on the other side of the lodge. The trail led up into the woods, but the Aldens saw that there was a small sandy beach nearby. After they had walked for a few minutes, Nora turned down a smaller trail, walked a few steps, and said, "There's your cabin. You're in Cabin Number Three, also known as Black Bear Cabin. There are seven cabins in all and four guest rooms in the lodge."

"Bears?" said Jessie.

"I read about the bears in my book about the Adirondacks," said Violet. "The book said that the bears won't hurt people. They're just as afraid of people as the people are of them."

"That's true, Violet," said Nora. "If you don't bother the bears, they won't bother you. In fact, that's true of all of this wilderness. The motto of the Adirondack Park is 'Forever Wild.' That means that these mountains are the homes for the animals and that the people are the guests. As guests you should be just as thoughtful and well behaved as you would be when you visit anybody's home."

Benny giggled. "If I see a bear, I'll say, 'Please, go away.' "

"I wonder what the bear will say?" Nora smiled at Benny. "Here we are." She pushed open the door of the cabin.

The Aldens stepped inside. The cabin was small, with windows at the front that looked out onto a screened porch above the lake.

Henry and Benny put their belongings in one of the smaller bedrooms and Violet and Jessie put theirs in the other. Grandfather took his suitcases to a larger bedroom. When they came back out into the living room, Nora was standing by the sink. "None of the cabins has plumbing — no running water," she explained. "This is the pump. You move the handle up and down and it pumps up water from the well for you to use. There's also an outside shower that uses water that runs down a pipe from the stream. But be careful! The stream water is *cold*."

"That's much nicer than our boxcar," said Violet. "We didn't even have a pump."

"The cabins don't have electricity, either," Nora said. "We use special lamps with candles for light. There is a woodstove and a fireplace, of course."

"We used to cook over a fire when we lived in the boxcar," Henry said.

"We'll cook on the stove," said Grandfather, "but we'll also eat many of our meals at the lodge."

"I like this place," said Violet.

"I'm glad," said Nora. "Some people think it is not modern enough and too far from other people, but I like it. I've been coming here since I was a little girl. I inherited it recently from my cousin."

"It's great," Henry said.

Nora smiled. "I think so, too. And there *is* electricity and plumbing at the lodge. Plus a small library and all kinds of games and puzzles. Lots of people like to spend the evenings by the fire at the lodge, doing puzzles or drinking hot chocolate." She smiled. "We usually build a fire in the fireplaces at night, even in the summer. Evenings in the mountains can get cool."

Grandfather looked at his watch. "After we get unpacked, we should be able to take a short hike before dinner."

"Why don't you take the Lakeside Trail," suggested Nora. "It branches off from the cabin trail just past your cabin. It's well marked and it will take you all the way around the lake."

"I'd like that," said Jessie.

"I'd like dinner," said Benny. He was always hungry.

Nora said, "Don't worry, Benny. You'll be

back in plenty of time for dinner. And if you see the Wild Man of the Woods, tell him hello for me."

"The Wild Man of the Woods!" exclaimed Violet. She looked alarmed. "Who is he?"

But Nora only smiled mysteriously. "You'll see," she promised.

CHAPTER 2

The Wild Man of the Woods

"What's that?" gasped Violet. She moved closer to her older sister.

"Don't worry, Violet. It's just a chipmunk. See?" said Jessie. She pointed.

"Oh," said Violet in a relieved voice.

"Hold on tightly to Watch's leash," Grandfather reminded Benny. "We don't want him to chase any of the animals."

"Especially the bears," agreed Benny.

"Woof," Watch barked, wagging his tail and looking at the chipmunk.

"No, Watch," said Benny. "Come on."

Watch gave the chipmunk one last, longing look and then trotted just ahead of Benny as they hiked around Lake Lucille. At first they passed several trails leading down to the lake and the other cabins. But soon they didn't see any trails at all except the one they were on. It went over rocks and around huge trees. It crossed a narrow stream that tumbled down the mountain into the lake. Through the trees and underbrush they could see glimpses of the lake down below.

"Look," said Henry. "If we stand on this big flat rock we can look out over the whole lake."

"Be careful," Grandfather warned.

Cautiously the Aldens stepped out onto the flat rock. Lake Lucille was spread out before them.

Benny pointed. "Look," he said. "There's Lucille Lodge across the lake."

"We're halfway around, then," said Jessie.

Suddenly Benny pointed again. "Look at that!" he exclaimed. "Is that a big fish down there?"

"Where?" asked Henry. He looked in the direction Benny was pointing. But he didn't see anything except a few ripples on the mirror-smooth surface of the lake.

"It could be a fish. Or it could be an underground stream bubbling up into the lake," said Grandfather Alden.

"Or it could be a monster," said a gravelly voice behind them.

The Aldens all turned around quickly in surprise. Watch barked loudly and pulled at his leash.

Standing behind them on the trail was a man in faded clothes of brown and green that seemed to match the woods. A wide-brimmed hat was pulled low over his short grizzled gray hair. He had a deeply tanned and lined face. In one hand he held a walking stick made of a whittled branch. A deep basket woven of strips of bark was slung over his shoulders. Next to him stood an enormous dog with short brown and silvery white fur and one blue eye and one brown eye.

"Who are you?" demanded Jessie.

"It's the Wild Man of the Woods!" cried Violet, shrinking back against her grandfather.

"Wild Man of the Woods? So you've heard about the Wild Man, eh?" said the man. His voice sounded like a growl.

Beside the man, the dog slowly wagged his tail and looked up at him.

"Nora told us about you," said Benny. "Shhh, Watch! Stop barking."

"Are you the Wild Man?" asked Henry.

The man shook his head. "My name's Carl Nielson." His teeth showed briefly in what might have been a smile. "I live up on the mountain, but I'm not the Wild Man."

"Who is, then?" asked Jessie.

Carl reached down and patted his dog's head. "He is. That's his name. Wildman."

Everyone stared for a moment. Then Benny started to laugh. "Oh, that's a joke," he said.

"Nora had us all fooled," said Grandfather Alden. "We're glad to meet you and Wildman, Mr. Nielson." He stepped forward to shake hands.

Mr. Nielson looked down at Grandfather's outstretched hand. Slowly, reluctantly, he shifted his walking stick to the other hand and shook hands with Mr. Alden. "You can call me Carl," he said. "Everybody calls me that."

"What did you mean about a monster, Carl?" asked Jessie.

"The monster that lives in the lake," said Carl.

"A *monster* lives in the lake? Oh, no," gasped Violet.

"Some say yes, some say no," said Carl. "I'd say yes."

Looking up at Carl, Benny said, "Have you seen the monster?"

"That's another story," said Carl. "I've got a delivery to make." Without saying good-bye, he walked away from them down the trail in the direction from which they had come. In a moment, he'd disappeared from sight.

"What a strange man," said Violet softly.

"I don't think he liked us," said Benny. "But I liked his dog. Maybe you and Wildman can play together sometime, Watch."

Watch wagged his tail.

"You don't think there is really a monster in the lake, do you, Grandfather?" asked Jessie.

"Well, some people believe that a monster lives in Lake Champlain," said Grandfather. "It's not all that far from here. They call him Champ."

"And don't forget Nessie. She's the monster who is supposed to live in Loch Ness in Scotland," said Henry.

"Well, I don't believe in monsters," said Jessie firmly.

"I know someone who might turn into a hungry monster if we don't get back to the lodge for dinner," teased Grandfather.

"Me," said Benny, forgetting about the lake monster. "Let's go!"

After putting Watch in Black Bear Cabin and giving him his dinner and some fresh water, the Aldens went quickly down the trail toward Lucille Lodge. They walked into the lodge through a narrow entrance hall with thick carpets on the floor. Doors opened off either side of the entrance hall. One door had a sign on it that said LIBRARY. The other door had a sign that said TELE-PHONE.

They went through the entrance into the great room. It had a high ceiling and an enormous fireplace on one side with big, comfortable chairs pulled up around it. On the other side of the room was the registration desk.

The dining room in Lucille Lodge had two huge fireplaces. At a small table near one of the fireplaces, a young woman with very short black hair was reading a book and eating slowly without really looking at what she ate. Every few minutes she put down her fork and picked up a pencil and made a note in the book.

"Hello," Nora greeted them as they walked into the dining room. "You can sit anywhere you'd like. The menu is on the blackboard on the wall over there. I'll come take your order in a few minutes."

The Aldens chose a table on the porch.

When Nora came to take their order, she said, "I can recommend the trout. I know it's fresh. Carl caught it and brought it today."

"That's the delivery he was going to make!" Jessie whispered to Violet.

Henry said, "Carl Nielson?"

"Oh, did you meet Carl?" asked Nora, her eyes twinkling.

"We met Carl *and* Wildman," Jessie told her.

"It was a good joke," Benny said. "Violet was afraid we were going to meet a real Wild Man of the Woods. Weren't you, Violet?"

"Maybe a little," Violet admitted, smiling.

"Carl told us about a monster, too," Jessie said. "A monster who lives in Lake Lucille."

The twinkle disappeared from Nora's eyes. "That's ridiculous! I don't understand why Carl picked this summer to make up all these crazy stories about a monster in the lake," she said. "He's going to hurt my business if he's not careful."

"Then there is no monster that lives in

Lake Lucille?" asked Violet, looking relieved.

"Of course not," said Nora. "In all the years I've been coming to this lake, I've never seen or heard anything that even remotely resembled a monster!"

She turned and walked quickly away, looking upset.

"I guess there isn't a monster," said Benny, a little disappointed. "But why would Carl make it up?"

"I don't know, Benny," said Henry. "Maybe he was just trying to scare us."

"Maybe. After all, he didn't seem to like us very much," said Jessie.

Violet said thoughtfully, "But what if Carl isn't making up the story about the monster? What if Nora is just pretending that it isn't true, so people won't be afraid to come stay at the lodge?"

Henry said, "The lodge has a small library, remember? Maybe we can go visit it after dinner."

"Yes," said Jessie. "We can see if we can find out anything about Champ and Nessie.

That might help us figure out if the monster in Lake Lucille is real."

After dinner, Grandfather took a cup of coffee into the great room and the Alden children went to the small library.

"Look," said Jessie. "There's an old set of encyclopedias."

"We can read all about monsters in there, can't we?" asked Benny.

"Monsters?" A tall, thin teenage boy with long black hair and dark brown eyes who had been slouched in an armchair in one corner of the library sat up. He looked scornfully at the Aldens. Then he shrugged. "Oh, well, I guess lots of little kids believe in monsters."

Henry's cheeks flushed. "We're not little kids. And we don't believe in monsters."

"Jason, Mom and Dad and I are here. It's time for dinner," said a girl's voice.

The Aldens turned to see a girl who was about Violet's or Jessie's age standing in the doorway of the library. Like Jason, she had black hair and brown eyes. Her hair was

pulled back in a long dark braid. She gave the Aldens a friendly smile. "Hi, I'm Nicole. Nicole Dubois. We're staying with my mom and dad in Moose Cabin for the whole summer. Who are you?"

"I'm Henry Alden, and these are my sisters, Jessie and Violet, and my brother, Benny," said Henry. "We just got here. We're in Black Bear Cabin."

"I'm glad you're here," said Nicole. "Now I'll have someone to do things with. Jason never wants to do anything but sit in the library and read. And the only other person staying here is Dr. Lin. She is a biologist who is doing research."

"There's nothing to do here *except* read," said the boy. "This place is *so* boring."

"It's not boring, Jason!" Nicole cried. "It's fun to hike and swim and fish and take the canoe out on the lake."

"Little kid stuff," said Jason with a yawn. He stood up and walked out of the room. "Anything would be better than being here — even summer school."

Nicole rolled her eyes. "He's going to

college this fall," she said. "Suddenly he thinks he's so grown-up."

"Most grown-ups don't act like *that*," Jessie blurted out. Then she stopped, embarrassed. "Sorry," she said.

"That's okay," said Nicole. "I have to go to dinner, but maybe I'll see you tomorrow."

"Okay," said Henry.

"We're in the library to do research on the monster," Benny said suddenly. "Do you believe in monsters?"

Nicole's eyes widened. She stepped forward. "You've heard about Lucy?" she asked in a low voice.

"Lucy?" asked Violet.

"The monster of Lake Lucille," said Nicole.

"Have you seen her?" asked Jessie. "Have you seen Lucy?"

Nicole whispered, "No, I haven't. But I know someone who has."

CHAPTER 3

Here Be Monsters?

"Who?" Jessie asked.

"Nicole, come on," a woman's voice said.

"I can't tell you right now. I have to go. But I'll tell you all about it tomorrow. Meet me at the beach tomorrow morning!" Nicole said in a low, rapid voice. Then she ran out the library door.

"So the monster *is* real," said Violet. "Oh, no!"

"We'd better get to work doing research," said Henry. "The more we know, the better."

The Aldens searched for information in the lodge's library for a long time. But the library was small, so they didn't find very much.

"We should go," said Benny the next morning when he had finished his big breakfast in the lodge dining room.

"Whoa. Where do you want to go in such a hurry?" asked Grandfather.

"To the beach," said Benny.

Grandfather took a sip of coffee. "Don't go in the water until I get there," he said. "There's no lifeguard."

"Okay," said Benny.

The Aldens put on their bathing suits, put on T-shirts and shorts, picked up their towels, and went down to the beach. At one end of the half-moon of shore was a small dock with four canoes pulled up onto the land next to it. At the other end Nicole sat waiting for them.

She jumped up when she saw them. "You're here at last!" she cried dramatically.

"Have you seen Lucy?" asked Benny. He

put his hand up to shade his eyes and peered out at the lake.

"No. But Carl Nielson has!" said Nicole.

"Carl Nielson? We met him yesterday," said Henry. "He's the one who told us about Lucy."

Nicole's face fell. "Really? So you know all about what happened," she said.

"No," Jessie said. "He just told us about Lucy. He wouldn't tell us if he had seen her or not."

"And then Nora told us there was no monster," added Violet.

"Nora's saying that because she's afraid the monster will scare away the guests at Lucille Lodge," said Nicole.

"Not many people are staying here," observed Henry. "Maybe they are scared to come visit."

"Maybe," said Nicole. She shrugged. "I wish *I* could see the monster, like Carl did."

"Where did he see it?" asked Henry.

"What did it look like?" asked Jessie at the same time.

"Did it chase him?" Benny chimed in.

"Over by the big rock across the lake. It had a small head and a long neck and a sort of hump on its back. He was in his boat fishing and it *tried to turn him over*."

"How did he escape?" asked Violet, horrified.

"He threw Lucy all of his fish. While she was eating them, he rowed back to shore and jumped out of the boat. When he looked back, Lucy was gone," Nicole told them.

"Maybe she wasn't trying to turn him over," said Benny. "Maybe she was just trying to play."

"Well, I don't want to ever play with a monster," said Nicole. "But I'd like to see her!"

"Me too," said Benny.

"I would, too," said Jessie, and Henry nodded.

Violet said, "Maybe I wouldn't."

"But Violet, if we could see her, we could prove she exists," Henry argued.

Violet didn't look convinced. "I don't know," she said. "Lots of people have seen

Nessie and Champ and that didn't prove that they were real."

"Nessie and Champ?" asked Nicole. She listened carefully as the Aldens explained what they had read.

"We thought we should do some research," Jessie concluded.

"Research . . ." repeated Henry, looking thoughtful, "research." Then he snapped his fingers. "I've got it! We have to have proof that the monster exists. Scientific proof."

"But how do we do that?" asked Jessie.

"I'm not sure," said Henry. "But maybe we could ask Dr. Lin."

"Because she's a scientist?" asked Benny.

"That's right, Benny," his brother answered.

Violet said, "But we don't know Dr. Lin. What if she doesn't want to help us?"

Nicole spoke up. "She's not very friendly."

"We won't know until we try," said Jessie. "Where is she staying, Nicole?"

"In Elk Cabin," said Nicole. "She picked the last one at the very end."

"Come on, then," said Jessie. "Let's go."

Dr. Lin was just coming out of her cabin as the Aldens walked up the trail to her door. The Aldens remembered seeing her reading in the dining room.

"Hello," called Henry.

"What are you doing here?" she asked. She closed the door behind her. She was wearing khaki hiking shorts, heavy socks, heavy boots, a long-sleeved T-shirt, and a cap. She had a pack on her back, and a camera and a pair of binoculars around her neck.

"We wanted to ask you a few questions," Jessie said.

"About what?" Dr. Lin asked. "Who are you?"

"We're the Aldens. We're here for a visit. And this is Nicole — " Henry began to say, but Dr. Lin interrupted.

"Never mind. I know who Nicole is. And I don't need to know who the rest of you are. I haven't got time." Dr. Lin pushed past them and started walking up the path away from her cabin.

"Wait," said Benny. "It's important. It's about the monster."

Dr. Lin stopped. Slowly she turned. "Did you say 'monster'?"

"Yes. The one Carl Nielson says he saw," Nicole said. "Do you know anything about it?"

"Why would I?" asked Dr. Lin, frowning. She started to turn away. "Besides, monsters don't exist."

Henry said quickly, "But if you wanted to prove that one did exist, how would you do it? Scientifically, I mean."

That surprised Dr. Lin. "Oh," she said. "Hmmm. Well, you'd need evidence. Scientific evidence. Castings of the tracks of the animal. A photograph. Tufts of fur. Or the animal itself."

"Alive?" asked Benny doubtfully.

Dr. Lin shrugged. "If possible . . . but I can't tell you how to catch a monster. I have serious field research to do."

She turned again and walked quickly up the trail.

The Aldens and Nicole looked at one another. Nicole said, "I have my camera. But we have to find the monster to make a picture."

"It might be easier to find Lucy's tracks," said Henry. "But what's a casting?"

"We can go back to the library at the lodge," suggested Jessie. "Maybe we can look it up there."

"Here," said Henry. "This book talks about how to make casts of animal tracks. You can use all kinds of materials — like wax. You melt it into the track and when it hardens, you have a cast of the animal's footprint."

Jessie read over Henry's shoulder. "Listen to this! It says that you can tell all kinds of things from a footprint — like how tall the animal is and whether it walks on two legs or four."

"We have *lots* of wax," said Benny excitedly. "We have all those candles in our cabin."

Violet nodded and took the book back to its place on the shelf.

Just then, they heard angry voices outside the half-open door of the library.

"I don't care, Drew. That's one of the best things about Lucille Lodge. It's not some fancy tourist hotel. The people who come here really love the mountains. They don't come to watch TV and order room service."

"Nora, be reasonable. We need to attract more business. And the way to do that is to modernize. Tear down the cabins and build new ones that have running water and — "

"No. We have enough business. We have enough money to live on. What more do we want?" Nora asked.

Drew said, "You're impossible."

"If you want more money, I'm surprised you didn't think we should sell it when we got that offer," Nora asked.

"Maybe we should have," Drew snapped. They heard heavy footsteps stomp away. Then they heard Nora sigh and walk slowly after her husband.

CHAPTER 4

A Sound in the Dark

When they were sure that Nora and Drew were gone, the Aldens and Nicole came cautiously out of the library.

"Are they going to sell Lucille Lodge?" asked Benny.

"I hope not, Benny," said Violet.

"If we catch the monster, it won't get a chance to scare away business," said Benny. "Then Nora won't have to sell the lodge."

"First we have to prove there is a monster," said Jessie.

"Or that there isn't one," Violet said.

"But if there isn't a monster," asked Nicole, "why is Carl saying that there is one?"

"It's part of the mystery," said Henry. He smiled. "And we like mysteries."

"Yes. We've solved a lot of them," said Benny. "Let's hurry and get the candles so we can solve this one!"

But although the Aldens and Nicole spent the whole day looking around the lake, they didn't see a single sign of Lucy.

They did find Carl again, however, just before it was time to go back to the lodge for dinner — or rather, Carl found them. He appeared as silently and unexpectedly as he had the day before.

"What are you looking for? Did you lose something?" he growled. They looked up from their search along the shoreline to see Carl and Wildman standing in the shadow of a huge tree.

"Hi," said Benny. "We're looking for monster tracks."

"Monster tracks? And have you found any?" asked Carl.

"No," said Benny. "We found all kinds of

tracks, but none of them are monster tracks. At least, I don't think they are."

"Here are some tracks," said Violet. She pushed aside a low branch that overhung the lake.

Carl walked closer and glanced down. "Raccoon," he said. "They're nocturnal animals. That means they mostly come out at night."

"Like owls?" asked Benny.

"Yes. And opossums. Deer, now, they move around most in the early morning and the early evening."

"Is Lucy a night creature or a day creature?" asked Violet.

"Why would I know that?" asked Carl.

"Because you've seen her," said Nicole.

"Seen who?" Carl asked.

"The lake monster — Lucy," said Nicole. "You told me so. Remember?"

"That's right. Nicole told us about how you escaped," Jessie said. "Did that happen at night or in the morning?"

"In the early morning it was," said Carl at last.

"If we were going to set a trap to catch Lucy," said Henry, "how would we do that?"

"Well, instead of setting a trap, my suggestion would be to take a picture of her," said Carl. "Good luck to you. Come, Wildman." As before, the man and the dog seemed to almost melt away and disappear into the trees.

"Found any monsters yet?" Jason asked with a sneer as the Aldens walked past his family's table after finishing dinner at the lodge that night.

"No. Not yet," said Benny.

"Well, don't stop looking. At least it keeps Nicole from bothering me all day long," said Jason.

Nicole made a face at her brother.

"See you tomorrow, Nicole," said Jessie.

"Right," said Nicole.

"Jason's going to be sorry he was mean to us and to his sister when we find Lucy," said Benny.

"If Lucy really does live in Lake Lucille,"

Violet said. "After all, Dr. Lin said that it wasn't possible, and she ought to know. She's a scientist."

"Even scientists aren't always right, you know," said Grandfather Alden. "Not too long ago, scientists said that the idea of traveling in space was nothing but science fiction. And you see how wrong they were."

Henry said, "That's true. We have to keep open minds until we can prove that Lucy does exist — or that she doesn't."

"But if she's not real, then why would Carl say that he saw her?" asked Benny.

"It's a two-part mystery," said Jessie as they reached the door of their cabin. "One: does a monster live in the lake and how do we prove that she does? Two: if we prove there is no monster, why did Carl say he saw one?"

Watch came running up to them, wagging his tail happily.

"Let's take Watch for one more walk before bed," suggested Henry.

"Good idea," said Grandfather Alden. He handed Henry the flashlight he had been carrying. "Everyone take a flashlight." Grandfather had taken a flashlight with him to dinner in case they had needed it on the walk home. But they hadn't, since the summer days were long. Now, however, it was getting dark fast.

Benny attached Watch's leash to his collar.

"We won't go far," Jessie told their grandfather. "Just a little way along the Lakeside Trail, and then we'll come back."

The Aldens went out into the night. Stars shone brightly above. A faint breeze brushed the leaves on the trees.

"I like it here," declared Violet. "Even if there is a monster in the lake."

Jessie said slowly, "You know, I've been thinking. Maybe it isn't a two-part mystery. Maybe it's a three-part mystery."

"What do you mean?" asked Benny. "What's part three?"

"Maybe Carl really did think he saw a monster. But it wasn't a monster. Maybe someone is trying to make everyone believe there is a monster in Lake Lucille."

"But who would do a mean thing like that?" asked Violet.

Just then they heard a long, low sound.

"What's that?" said Benny, stopping in his tracks. Watch looked toward the lake.

"Look at Watch," said Jessie. "It came from the — "

The noise came again, a sound almost like the mooing of a cow, but more eerie. Watch barked once, sharply, and pulled on his leash, straining to get down to the water.

"It's coming from the lake," said Henry. "Let's go." He raced as fast as he dared back along the main trail and turned down the first trail that led to the lake — the one that went right past Dr. Lin's cabin.

Just as they reached the beach, the long, low sound came again. Henry shone his flashlight out over the water and the sound faded away.

"What was that?" asked Violet.

"I don't know," said Jessie. "But it sounded as if it came from out in the lake."

"Do you think someone is out there?" asked Benny.

"Someone. Or some*thing*," answered Jessie.

Just then an angry voice behind them said, "What is going on here?"

The Aldens turned to see Dr. Lin standing on the edge of the beach at the foot of the trail that led down past her cabin. She was wearing sneakers and a bathrobe over her pajamas and holding a flashlight in one hand.

"Dr. Lin!" exclaimed Henry. "What are you doing here?"

"I asked you first," said Dr. Lin crossly. "But if you want to know what *I* am doing here, I came out to investigate why a herd of noisy children would run past my cabin in the middle of the night."

"It's not the middle of the night," cried Benny. He paused. "Is it?"

"For me it might as well be. I go to bed very early because I get up early to do my work," said Dr. Lin. "I was sound asleep when you came crashing by."

"I'm sorry," said Henry. "We didn't mean to wake you up."

"We heard a noise from the lake," said Jessie.

"And we wanted to see what it was," Violet finished.

"A noise? What noise?" Dr. Lin cocked her head to listen. Everyone stood very still, even Watch. For a long moment no sound could be heard at all except the whisper of the wind through the trees. Then faintly and far away they heard hooting.

"Oh, that," said Dr. Lin. "That's just a mother bear and her cub calling back and forth to one another."

"It sounds like an owl," said Benny.

"It does sound that way a little bit," Dr. Lin agreed. She didn't seem so angry now. She gave Benny a little smile. "I remember the first time I heard the bears calling to each other. I wasn't much older than you are. I think that's when I decided to become a biologist. But you don't have anything to worry about. Those bears are very far away. They won't bother you."

She turned to go.

"Wait," Jessie blurted out. "That's not the sound we heard. It was more like a mooing sound, only lower and more growly."

Dr. Lin looked over her shoulder with a frown. "I've never heard a noise like that. There's no animal I know of that makes that sound in these mountains. Or anywhere, for that matter. It must have been the wind blowing. . . ."

Her voice trailed off as the long, low sound rolled across the lake once more.

CHAPTER 5

A Monster Hunt

"What was that?" asked Jessie after the sound had died away. "What kind of animal makes a sound like that?"

Dr. Lin looked very puzzled and surprised. "I don't know," she said. "I've never heard an animal call like that one."

Benny was very excited. "Dr. Lin! Dr. Lin!" he exclaimed. "Do you think it could have been Lucy? The monster in the lake?"

"No, I don't," Dr. Lin answered firmly. "There is no such thing as a lake monster — not here, not in Lake Champlain, not in

Loch Ness. It is scientifically impossible."

"Then what made that sound?" asked Violet.

"I don't know," said Dr. Lin. "But whatever made it, I'm sure there is a simple explanation." She tightened the sash on her bathrobe and turned away again. "It's late and I'm going to bed."

She turned her flashlight onto the trail, following its beam through the trees. A few minutes later they heard the door of her cabin slam shut.

"Now, who could that be knocking at the door so early in the morning?" asked Grandfather Alden the next day.

The Aldens had just finished eating breakfast and were washing the dishes and putting them away. Benny dropped a handful of spoons in the drawer and said, "I'll find out."

A moment later he opened the door and Nicole burst in. "Did you hear it?" she gasped. "Did you hear that sound on the lake last night?"

"The bears calling to each other?" Jessie asked cautiously.

"No! I know what the bears sound like. This was a completely different sound. Kind of like a weird cow," said Nicole.

"Yes!" cried Benny. "We heard and Watch heard and Dr. Lin heard. Grandfather heard, too!"

Nicole clapped her hands together. "I knew it! I knew it! It's got to be Lucy," she said.

"Dr. Lin says it's not really an animal. She said there's some 'simple explanation,'" Henry said, repeating what the biologist had said to them the night before.

"What we need to find out is what made that sound," said Jessie.

"Or who," said Violet.

Jessie nodded. Nicole said, "I know. Let's see if we can take a canoe out on the lake. Maybe we can find something that way."

"Even if we don't, it sounds like fun," said Henry.

"We have to go tell someone at the

lodge that we want to use the canoes," said Nicole. "And get life jackets."

When the Aldens and Nicole reached the lodge, Nora was at the registration desk talking to a young man and woman holding suitcases. "I think you'll like it here in the lodge. Your room is called Lakeview. It's the second room on the right at the top of the stairs," she said, handing the young woman a key.

"Thanks," said the young woman. The couple went up the stairs.

Nora turned. "Hi," she said, smiling. "What can I do for you kids?"

"We'd like to take out two of the canoes and we need life jackets," said Jessie.

"Good idea. It's a beautiful day for a paddle around the lake," said Nora. "Come on. I keep the life jackets in our storage house."

She led them out of the lodge to a low building next to it. Pushing open the door, she removed several life jackets in various sizes from hooks on the wall. The building was filled with all kinds of tools.

"Wow," Henry said admiringly. "This is better than a hardware store."

Nora laughed. "We're a long way from any hardware store out here. Drew or I only go to town once a week, on Thursdays, for supplies. We have to be prepared to fix things ourselves. And you can't do that without the proper tools."

"Look at these old horns with the balloons on one end," said Benny.

"Benny, wait," Nora began, but it was too late. Benny had picked up one of the horns and squeezed it. A blast of sound made Benny drop the horn to cover his ears. Watch yelped in surprise.

"Owww," said Benny. "What was that?" He took his hands away from his ears.

Nora picked up the horn. "It's an air horn, Benny," she told him. "We have it in case we need to signal for someone out on the lake.

"And speaking of the right tools . . ." Nora went on. She reached up and took a very small life jacket off a hook. "We even have a life jacket for dogs."

"Watch knows how to swim," said Benny.

"Yes, and so do you, Benny, but you know that you are always supposed to wear your life jacket when you are in a boat," Henry said.

"I know," said Benny. "Come on, Watch. I'll help you put your life jacket on."

"By the way, you didn't hear any noises coming from the lake last night, did you?" asked Jessie, trying to sound casual.

"No," said Nora quickly — almost too quickly, Jessie thought. Nora added, "Well, you'd better get started if you want to enjoy paddling around the lake before it gets too hot. Just leave the life jackets on their hooks when you are finished. The door is usually unlocked."

She turned and walked quickly back to the lodge. Jessie stared thoughtfully after her.

"What is it, Jessie?" asked Henry.

"Nora didn't even ask what kind of noise, or when we might have heard it — or why I was asking," said Jessie.

"Do you think she did hear the noise and

doesn't want anyone to know?" asked Violet.

"It's possible," said Jessie. "Especially if she thinks it could be bad for business."

"There is only one thing to do," Henry declared.

"What?" asked Nicole.

"Go find Lucy — or whatever was making that noise," said Henry.

When the Aldens and Nicole got back to the beach, they saw Jason stretched out on a towel in the sand. He was wearing his bathing suit and reading. He had on dark glasses and a baseball hat pulled down over his eyes.

"Hi," said Benny.

"Mmm," said Jason without raising his gaze from his book.

"Want to come with us on a canoe trip around the lake?" asked Henry politely.

Jason glanced up. "Oh. Are you going to look for monsters?" He laughed.

Violet said, "Even if we don't see Lucy, it will be fun."

"Thanks anyway," said Jason, "but I'll stay here." He pointed to the camera that Nicole was holding and added, "When you take Lucy's picture, tell her to smile." He rolled over on one side and kept reading.

Henry, Benny, and Watch got into one canoe. Jessie, Nicole, and Violet took the other. They paddled out into the deep blue lake. The water was very still.

When they were in the middle of the lake, they heard the hum of a car motor from the direction of the lodge.

"Sound travels far across the water," commented Jessie.

Violet raised the binoculars she had brought along and trained them on the lodge. "Someone just drove up to the lodge," she reported.

A door slammed.

"That's Drew, coming out of the front door of the lodge. Now a woman in khaki pants and a plaid shirt is getting out of the car. She and Drew are shaking hands," Violet said.

"It's probably another guest," said Nicole.

"I don't see any luggage," said Violet. "Wait! Nora just came out of the lodge. She's got her hands on her hips. She looks angry. It looks as if she and Drew are arguing."

Everyone in the canoe turned to squint at the lodge. But although they could see the building, without the binoculars they couldn't see much else.

A car door slammed. Then the lodge door slammed once, then again. The car motor started, then faded away.

"What happened now?" cried Benny.

"The woman in the plaid shirt gave Nora something and she threw it down. Then the woman got in her car and drove away, and Nora went back into the lodge. Drew followed her," Violet said. She lowered the binoculars.

"Wow, it's just like a play," Nicole exclaimed.

"Only you couldn't see it," Benny said.

"Would you like to use the binoculars?" Violet asked Nicole.

"Yes," said Nicole. "I think we should all

take turns using them. We can keep a look-out for Lucy."

"Good idea," Henry said.

They paddled on. They saw a squirrel drinking from the edge of the lake. They saw a hawk circling high above. But although they paddled around the lake all morning, they didn't see any sign of a lake monster.

The children put their life preservers back into the storage building. They were on their way to the cabin when Violet bent down and picked up a small rectangle of ivory-colored paper. "Look," she said.

"What is it, Violet?" asked Jessie.

"It's a business card," Violet told them. "'Mountain Home Real Estate,'" she read from the card. "'Geena Bush, Broker.'"

"That must be who came to visit Drew and Nora," said Nicole.

"I don't think she came to visit Nora," said Jessie thoughtfully. "Not if Nora was angry to see her."

"You're right," said Henry. "Nora doesn't want to sell Lucille Lodge. But Drew sounded as if he might when we overheard them arguing. Remember?"

"Did this broke lady get in trouble for coming to see Drew?" asked Benny.

"Broker, Benny," said Violet. "Yes, it looks as if she did. This card must be what she tried to give Nora and what Nora threw down."

Jessie said slowly, "If Lucy isn't real — and we haven't found any scientific proof that she is — do you suppose that Geena Bush could have something to do with the rumors . . . and with the sounds we heard last night?"

"Or Drew?" suggested Henry.

"But if Geena Bush had driven up to the lake last night, we would have heard her car. Remember how sounds carry across the lake?" said Nicole.

"True," said Jessie.

"What if Drew and Geena Bush are working together?" said Violet.

Henry nodded. "It could be. Maybe he sneaked out last night and hiked to one side of the lake to make the sound."

"What we need are more clues," said Jessie. "But how do we find them?"

"We keep looking," Benny said. "It's a mystery and we're good at solving mysteries. We will solve this one, too!"

The Aldens had finished dinner and were sitting on the screened porch of their cabin. A soft rain that had been falling for the last two hours had just stopped.

They were glad to sit on the cozy porch and rest. It had been a long hard day, and they were a little discouraged because they were no closer to solving the mystery of the lake monster. No one was talking very much.

"Grrr," Watch growled suddenly.

"What is it, Watch?" asked Violet.

Watch pressed his nose against the screened porch and peered down into the darkness. "Grrr," he growled again.

"Watch hears something, don't you,

boy?" asked Henry. He patted Watch's head. Watch wagged his tail, but he growled again.

"Maybe it's a bear," said Violet, sounding a little scared.

"I doubt that," Grandfather Alden said. "It is unlikely a bear would come this close to the cabin. More likely it is a raccoon or opossum. Or it could just be rain dripping from the leaves."

"But you have to stay inside, Watch, whatever it is," said Jessie. She paused. Then she said softly, "What if it is Lucy?"

Watch ran to the other end of the porch. He pressed his nose against the screen and peered intently into the night. He uttered a short, sharp bark and looked over his shoulder as if to say, *C'mon!*

Henry walked back through the cabin and picked up the largest flashlight from the table by the door. He went back to the porch and clicked it on, throwing a powerful beam out into the night.

In the beam of the flashlight, they could see trees and a glint of water and the lighter color of the lakeshore. But nothing was moving.

Henry turned the beam in the direction that Watch was now peering. No one could see anything.

"There's nothing in that direction, Watch, except the other cabins and the lodge," said Henry.

Watch stood on guard for a long moment after that. Then he turned and trotted back to Jessie and jumped up onto her lap. Henry clicked the flashlight off.

"Whatever it was, it's gone now," said Grandfather. He stood up and stretched and yawned. "Time for bed. I'm going to do a little fishing tomorrow and I want to get an extra-early start so I can be back in time for a late breakfast with you all."

"Yes, and we have work to do, too," said Benny.

"That's right, Benny," said Jessie. The Aldens went back into Black Bear Cabin to get ready for bed. Benny was the last one to leave the porch. He stared out through the screen, trying to see through the night to the lake.

"Benny," Henry called. "Come on. It's time for bed."

"Coming," answered Benny. He leaned close to the screen. "Good night, Lucy," he said softly before going inside to join his family.

CHAPTER 6

Enormous Footprints

"Benny? What are you doing up so early?" Jessie whispered the next morning.

"Are you awake?" asked Benny. He was dressed. Watch was standing beside Benny with his paws on the edge of Jessie's bed. He was staring at Jessie, and she noticed that his leash was attached to his collar and that Benny was holding the other end of it.

Jessie yawned and rubbed her eyes. She said, "I guess I am now."

"Good," said Benny. "Grandfather left a

little while ago to go fishing. That's when Watch and I woke up. Let's go down to the lake. We can see if we can find what Watch was barking at last night."

In the bunk across from Jessie, Violet mumbled something in her sleep and rolled over, pulling her covers up over her head.

"Shhh," said Jessie. She yawned again. "Whatever was out there is long gone, Benny . . . but okay. I'll meet you on the steps of the cabin in five minutes."

Jessie left a note saying where she and Benny had gone in case Violet and Henry woke up before they got back. She went outside and walked with Benny down the path that led from the cabin to the lake.

A faint mist rose from the water. The leaves were wet on the trail from the rain the night before. Drops of water rolled off the leaves they brushed against. The sun had not yet come up over the mountains to begin to dry up the puddles.

"Let's whisper," said Jessie. "Remember how sound carries? We don't want to wake up everybody on the whole lake."

Benny nodded. "Hear that, Watch?" he said.

Watch wagged his tail briefly and pulled on the leash. He was panting a little; he was excited.

The empty beach curved away from them. It was made of rocks and coarse sand. Benny, Watch, and Jessie walked slowly up and down the beach, but they didn't see any footprints. The rain had washed the shoreline clean.

"Maybe Watch heard a bird flying by," said Jessie. She stifled a yawn.

Just then, Watch began tugging hard on the leash. "What is it, Watch?" asked Benny. He let Watch lead him down the beach toward the canoes. Suddenly Watch veered off and pulled Benny toward a thick clump of bushes.

"Whoa. Slow down," said Benny.

Watch didn't slow down. He stopped and stared at the low bushes.

"Look," said Jessie. "Those bushes are all mashed and the branches are broken as if something big had crashed through them." She started forward to examine them. But Benny stopped her.

"Look." He gasped. "Look at those footprints!"

There was a trail of huge footprints on a smooth swath of sand just at the edge of the bushes.

Keeping a tight hold on Watch, Benny leaned cautiously forward. Jessie did, too.

The footprints weren't human. They had four long toes with webbing between them. The toes ended in claw marks. The prints were huge, easily a foot long.

"These are Lucy's footprints," said Benny, forgetting to whisper. "I know it!"

"They could be, Benny," said Jessie, forgetting to whisper, too.

"Then Lucy is *real*," said Benny. "I knew it! That's what Watch heard last night. It was Lucy!"

"We need to make a cast of a footprint as soon as possible," said Jessie. "And take a picture. Watch and I will stay here to guard the footprints and you go get Henry and Violet — and the wax candles we saved in case we found footprints."

"I'll be right back!" Benny promised.

He ran back to the cabin. Benny threw open the cabin door with a loud crash.

"Wake up!" he cried. "We've found Lucy!"

Henry ran out of the bedroom in his pajamas. His hair was sticking out all over his head. "What? What's wrong?" he asked Benny.

Violet ran out of her bedroom hopping on one foot and trying to pull a slipper onto the other. "What happened?" she said.

"Lucy," said Benny.

Violet looked quickly around as if she expected to see the lake monster in the cabin.

"Where?" asked Henry.

"Down by the lake. Bring the candles! Hurry!" Benny said.

"They're coming," he reported to Jessie as soon as he ran back to join her. A few minutes later, Henry and Violet came running out onto the beach. Violet had her camera around her neck.

"What is it?" Henry called breathlessly.

"Look," said Jessie. She stepped back and Benny pointed dramatically.

Violet and Henry stared. Then Violet said in a hushed voice, "Maybe there really *is* a lake monster."

"Yes," said Jessie, trying to sound calm.

Violet held the camera up and took a picture of one of the footprints. Then she took a photograph of the crushed bushes and broken twigs around it. Moving carefully, she took another photograph of the footprint from a different angle, and then another.

Jessie used a tape measure to measure one of the footprints. "This one's thirteen inches long," she said, "and seven and a half inches wide."

"That's big, isn't it?" asked Benny.

"Yes," answered Jessie.

Then Henry took the candles out and lit one. He used it to melt the other candles into the outline of a footprint. When he was finished, he had used up all the candles. Carefully he snuffed out the stub of the can-

dle he'd been using. He dipped the end of the match into the lake and put the match and candle into his pocket. He didn't want to start a fire — or be a litterbug.

"We have to let the wax harden now, before we lift the cast up," said Jessie.

"Maybe we should look for more clues," Violet suggested.

"Good idea," said Henry.

The four Aldens spread out and looked around carefully. They didn't see any more trampled bushes or broken limbs in the woods near the footprints.

"That means she didn't come from the woods," said Jessie.

They found several large rocks that had been knocked over and some sharp scratches in the sand that looked as if they had been made by claws. "She could have done that," said Henry.

"Yes," agreed Jessie. "But why did she come out of the water here? And why did she go back in?"

"Maybe when Watch growled, she heard him and it scared her," suggested Benny.

"But if Watch was growling at Lucy, why was he facing in the other direction part of the time when he was growling?" Jessie went on. "Remember? He went to the other end of the porch."

"Maybe Lucy was swimming away," said Henry. He checked the cast of the footprint. The wax had hardened. Very carefully, Henry lifted the wax out of the footprint. Sand and grit were embedded in the bottom of the cast. He held both hands under the enormous wax impression so that it wouldn't break.

Violet pulled some branches over all the footprints. "We should show them to Dr. Lin," she suggested.

"Yes," Jessie said. "But first let's take this cast up to the cabin and put it in a safe place," said Jessie. "We don't want anything to happen to it."

They took the cast up to the cabin and Jessie put it in the lower drawer of the bureau in the room she and Violet were sharing. Then, although it was early, they went to Dr. Lin's cabin.

But Dr. Lin wasn't there.

"I wonder where she is so early in the morning," said Violet.

Henry looked down at the wet grass in front of the cabin. "I don't know. But I don't think she's been here all night."

"Why?" asked Benny.

"Look at the wet grass," said Henry. "We made a trail through it when we walked up to the cabin door. But there was no trail before we got here."

"You're right!" Jessie said. "Do you think she's all right?"

"What if Lucy got her?" Violet said.

"Lucy wouldn't do that," said Benny.

"I'll write a note and we can leave it on her door," said Jessie. "I think we should talk to Dr. Lin before we do anything else. After all, she is a scientist."

"Yes," said Henry. "Maybe now that we have a cast of the footprint, she'll listen to us and help us solve this mystery."

CHAPTER 7

A Monster Bite

"This is good," said Benny. "I was hungry." He finished the last bite of his sandwich and looked over the picnic spread out on the flat rock by the lake.

The Aldens and Nicole were hiking around the lake again, looking for clues. The Aldens hadn't told anyone about the footprints except Nicole. They were still waiting for Dr. Lin to get back to her cabin. Nicole had told them that Dr. Lin often went away for overnight camping trips while she was doing research. "She always tells Nora," Nicole explained. "That's so if she gets lost, they'll know to go look for her."

"That's good," said Benny.

When they had run into Drew earlier, Benny had immediately told him of their plans to hike around the lake. "So if we get lost," he explained, "you'll know where to look."

Drew had nodded. "Good for you. You're already learning important lessons in wilderness safety," he said. "I'll tell Nora, too." He paused. "It *is* beautiful here," he said, almost to himself. Then he said, "Stop by the lodge before you go on your hike. I might have a surprise for you."

The surprise had been a picnic lunch that Drew had made especially for them.

Benny now picked up another peanut butter and jelly sandwich. "Drew is a great cook," he said happily.

"This is good," agreed Jessie. She was eating a sandwich stacked high with tomatoes, lettuce, and cheese, and a delicious pasta salad. "It was nice of him to make lunch for us. He even remembered Watch."

Hearing his name, Watch wagged his tail and kept on chewing on the giant dog biscuit that Drew had packed into the lunch in a brown paper bag that said FOR WATCH.

"I didn't like Drew at first," said Violet. "But now I think he's not so bad. It's hard to get used to a new place and new people. Maybe he's just shy." Violet could understand that. She was a little shy herself sometimes.

They ate in silence for a while. Then Nicole glanced out over the water. "Look," she said. "Someone has taken one of the canoes out on the lake."

Henry picked up the binoculars and peered through them. "It looks like your brother," he told Nicole.

"Jason? I don't believe it!" Nicole said.

Henry handed her the binoculars. Nicole peered through them and said in a surprised voice, "It *is* Jason. That's the first time this whole summer he has taken the canoe out. Maybe he's starting to like it here after — oh, no!"

"What?" asked Henry.

"His boat just turned over. We have to help him!" gasped Nicole.

She jumped up and began to run back along the trail toward a spot closer to the canoe. She was still holding the binoculars.

The Aldens jumped up, too. Looking out over the lake, they could see the bright green bottom of the canoe upended on the water.

Jessie squinted. "I think I see Carl."

"Come on," said Henry, "let's go help."

The Aldens ran after Nicole. Just as they caught up with her, they saw Carl and Jason wading out of the lake near the trail. Wildman stood on the shore, half in and half out of the water. He was barking.

"Jason, Jason, are you all right?" Nicole cried.

"Of course I'm all right," said Jason. He sounded angry. "I had a life jacket on and I can swim."

Carl growled, "Yes, but if you'd been hit on the head when you fell out of the canoe, it could have been worse for you."

Jason reached the shore and pulled his arm free from Carl. "I don't need your help," he said crossly.

Nicole said, "Jason, Carl helped you. He didn't know whether or not you were hurt. He went in the water after you. He saved your life. He's a hero!"

Carl's deeply tanned cheeks reddened. "None of that, now," he said. "I'm no hero. I did what anyone would have done if they saw someone fall out of a canoe."

"I didn't fall out of my canoe!" Jason almost shouted.

"Then what happened?" Jessie asked.

"Someone grabbed my paddle and pulled me out. And turned the canoe over!" Jason said. He held up the paddle angrily. "It happened too quickly for me to see who did it."

Everyone froze.

Then Violet said in a soft voice, "Jason, what happened to your paddle?"

Jason looked at the paddle for the first time. His eyes widened. He let go of the paddle, and it would have fallen except that Henry caught it.

The tip of the paddle looked as if someone — or something — had taken a huge bite out of it.

"Lucy!" gasped Nicole. "Lucy bit your paddle. Lucy turned your canoe over."

Carl stood as still as a statue. Now he seemed pale beneath his ruddy tan. "It's not possible," he whispered.

Jason recovered his wits. "You're right. It's not." He glared at Nicole. "Is this your idea of a joke?"

"A joke?" Nicole's voice rose. "A joke?" she repeated. "I would never do something like that."

"Besides, how could she?" Henry said reasonably. "She was with us."

"Maybe you're all in it together! Maybe you would do anything to prove that some phony monster is real," said Jason.

"We didn't turn you over! We were having a picnic," said Benny.

"Besides, none of us is wet," Jessie pointed out. "Even if one of us was able to swim out to your canoe and turn you over, we would be wet now."

"And we saw a footprint, too," cried Benny. "Of Lucy's. On the beach. She's real. It wasn't us who grabbed your paddle. It was Lucy."

Jason looked from one of them to the other. Then he said, "Somebody did this to me. And it wasn't the monster. In fact, the only monsters I see around here are you little kids."

With that, he turned and walked away. His sneakers made squishing sounds as he walked.

Carl still hadn't moved. His gaze was fixed on the paddle that Henry held. Then he began to shake his head slowly.

"Are you okay?" Jessie asked him.

Carl looked up. He seemed surprised, as if he hadn't expected to see them.

"Are you cold? We have a blanket with us. I could go get it for you," Violet volunteered.

"No, thank you," said Carl.

"You were right about the lake monster, Carl," said Henry.

"Yes, Lucy is *real*," said Benny. "No matter what Jason says. We had a footprint already. And now we have this paddle to prove it."

Carl gave Benny an odd look. Then, without speaking another word, he disappeared into the woods, with Wildman right behind him.

As they walked back to the lodge to return the napkins and blanket and thermoses from the picnic, they met Nora coming out of the storage building.

She frowned when she saw the Aldens and Nicole. "Jason told me what happened," she said. "Is this some kind of joke you kids are playing?"

"No," said Henry.

"There is no monster," said Nora. "I practically grew up on this lake. I know it. I would have known if there was anything like a monster in it. There isn't."

"Then what took a bite out of this?" asked Jessie, holding up the paddle.

"It got caught on a rock. Or a branch under the water," said Nora.

"Or bitten by a lake monster," said Nicole.

"Oh, my goodness! What happened to the paddle?" asked a woman's voice. It was the young woman who had checked into the lodge the day before.

"Nothing," said Nora. "Someone turned a canoe over in the lake. I'm about to paddle out and tow it home."

The man with the woman peered at the paddle. "It looks as if those are teeth marks," he said.

"They might be," said Benny. "They might have been made by the lake monster."

"Lake monster? What lake monster?" cried the woman, looking very alarmed.

At that moment Dr. Lin came hiking into the clearing in front of the lodge. "There you are," she said to the Aldens and Nicole. She held up the note Jessie had written. "What is all this about finding footprints left by the monster of Lake Lucille?"

CHAPTER 8

Suspects and Clues

"There is no monster!" Nora practically shouted.

"That does it," the man said. "We're checking out of here. We don't need to stay in a place where people think they have seen monsters."

"But — " Nora began.

"And we'll want a full refund," the man went on.

Nora's lips tightened. "Fine. I'll give it to you right now. Come on." Her chin held high, she led the couple back into the lodge.

"We have a paddle, too. Lucy bit it," said Benny.

Dr. Lin looked down at the paddle and raised her eyebrows. "It certainly looks as if something might have bitten it," she said. "Now why don't you show me these footprints you were talking about. The originals first, and then the cast."

Quickly they led the way back to the beach. "Right here," said Benny proudly. He pulled back the protective covering of branches that they had left over the footprints early that morning and pointed.

"Where?" asked Dr. Lin, squatting down.

Benny looked down. His eyes got big. His mouth turned down in disappointment.

The footprints were gone!

"They were here this morning!" Jessie cried. "We all saw them."

Dr. Lin stood up. "Well, whatever you saw, they're not here now."

"We still have the wax cast," said Violet.

"Yes. We can show you that. And we took photographs and measured it, too," said Henry.

But when Jessie took the wax cast of the giant foot out of her drawer and brought it into the main room of the cabin to show Dr. Lin, the scientist didn't look surprised or impressed at all.

She studied it thoughtfully. After a long moment she said, "It is very big and you did a nice job of making a cast of whatever this is."

"It's Lucy's footprint," said Benny.

"If it is, it is certainly a most unusual footprint," said Dr. Lin. "In all my studies, I have never come across any animal that had both the webbed feet of a duck and the enormous claws of a tiger. This footprint looks as if it were made by two entirely different species . . . or one. My guess is that it is only one species of animal."

"Which one?" asked Henry.

Dr. Lin looked up to meet his gaze. "Human," she said simply. "I'm sorry. I've said all along that the existence of a lake monster was not possible. This only proves me right."

With that, Dr. Lin turned and left the cabin.

"She's wrong," Benny burst out. "Lucy is real. I know she is."

"I don't know what to believe anymore, Benny," said Jessie. "We need some more information. We need to do some more research on Nessie and Champ and on the kinds of animals scientists think they might be."

"But how?" asked Violet.

"We're going to take a trip to town," said Jessie.

"To the library," guessed Henry.

"But how?" asked Violet.

"We'll get Nora or Drew to take us," said Jessie. "Remember what Nora told us? They go to town every Thursday. And tomorrow is Thursday."

That night at dinner, the Aldens asked Nora if they could get a ride to town the next day.

"To Saranac Lake?" asked Nora. "Sure. What for?"

"We want to go to the library," said Jessie.

To their relief, Nora didn't ask them why. She said, "I rely on library books to get me through the winters. Saranac Lake has a nice library."

After saying good-bye to Watch and Grandfather the next morning, the Aldens found themselves in the big old pickup truck with Drew. He didn't talk much as he drove. Instead he leaned forward, clenching the wheel tightly and staring at the road. Not until they had reached the outskirts of Saranac Lake did he relax.

"There's the post office," he said as he drove down the street. "And the hardware store. And over there is a bookstore. We've even got a health food store."

Drew sounded proud of the town — as if he lived there. "This town has a rich and interesting history," he went on. "A long time ago, people who were sick with a disease called tuberculosis used to come here to try to get well. Saranac Lake was famous for that. It was called 'taking the cure.' Robert Louis Stevenson, who wrote *Treasure Island*, stayed here for a time."

The Aldens were surprised. "I thought you didn't like it here," said Benny. "But you sound like you do."

Drew looked surprised and then a little embarrassed. "It grows on you," he said, almost as gruffly as Carl. "Here's the library. I'll meet you at the health food store in an hour."

The Aldens liked the library at Saranac Lake. They quickly found a book with more information about the Loch Ness Monster.

"Look. It says *loch* is the word they use in Scotland for 'lake,'" said Violet. "The two words do sort of sound the same."

Henry picked up another book. "And look at this," he said, keeping his voice low because they were in a library. "Here's a drawing of what the Loch Ness Monster is supposed to look like. Some people say she is related to a certain kind of dinosaur."

"Dinosaurs are extinct. Aren't they?" asked Benny.

"Yes," said Jessie.

Violet whispered, "Dr. Lin."

Her brothers and sister looked up.

"What?" asked Henry.

Holding up a piece of paper, Violet repeated, "Dr. Lin. Here's a piece of paper with her name at the top. See? It says, 'From the desk of Dr. Kisha Lin.' "

"Where did you get that, Violet?" asked Jessie.

"Out of this book. It was marking the place where I was reading about the Loch Ness Monster," said Violet.

The Aldens studied the piece of paper. "Look. It's a list of all the books that have information about Nessie and Champ," said Henry. "It looks as if Dr. Lin has been doing research on them, too."

As she peered at the paper, Violet said, "But look at the date on the piece of paper. If she was doing research on Nessie or Champ because of Lucy, it was weeks before we got here, at the very beginning of the summer."

"Why is Dr. Lin researching lake monsters," asked Jessie, "if she doesn't believe Lucy is real?"

*   *   *

As they walked back toward the health food store, the Aldens discussed what they had learned.

"If Lucy is real," said Violet, "why didn't Nora know anything about her? If she is a relative of a dinosaur, like some of the books thought Nessie might be, she would have had to be in Lake Lucille a very long time."

"True," Henry said.

"Maybe Nora did know about Lucy," said Violet. "Maybe she didn't want other people to know because she was afraid of driving away business."

Jessie shook her head. She said, "I hate to say this, but if Lucy had been around for very long, other people would know about her. There would be stories and legends, just like there are about Nessie and Champ."

"If Lucy's not real, who is making her real?" asked Benny.

"That's a good question, Benny," Henry said. "Who wants us to believe that Lucy is real, and why?"

"Drew," said Violet. "He wants to sell Lucille Lodge and leave. Maybe he's trying to scare Nora into agreeing. Or scare off so many people that they go out of business and have to sell the lodge."

"Maybe. I'm not so sure about that," said Henry. "But you are right. We have to count Drew as a suspect."

"And Geena Bush," said Violet. "She wants to buy Lucille Lodge."

"Of course she's a suspect. And of course she and Drew might be working together," Jessie said.

"Don't forget Carl," said Henry. "Remember what Nora said when we first told her about the monster. 'I don't understand why Carl picked this summer to make up all these crazy stories about a monster in the lake?' "

"But why would Carl want to scare people away?" asked Violet.

"Carl doesn't like many people, I think," said Benny. "Maybe that's why."

"Yes," agreed Jessie. "And Carl knows the

mountains better than anybody. It would be easy for him to sneak up on shore in the night and leave a fake footprint."

"And make fake monster calls in the night," said Benny.

"And he was right there when the canoe turned over. Maybe he did it," said Henry. "Maybe that's how he got wet — turning over the canoe, not trying to save Jason."

"But don't forget, he was *shocked* when he saw the bite in the paddle," Jessie said.

"He was," Violet agreed. "I don't think he was just pretending."

"What about Dr. Lin?" asked Henry.

"But she's never believed Lucy is real," said Violet.

"She could be saying that to keep from seeming suspicious. She could be trying to make everyone think there is a monster, because then she could write a paper on it. It would make her famous," said Jessie.

"She's pretty familiar with the woods around here from her research," said Violet. "She could have done all those things herself."

"But where was she when the canoe turned over?" asked Benny. "We didn't see her anywhere."

"She could have swum away while everybody was looking at Jason," suggested Henry.

Jessie looked doubtful. "Maybe," she said.

They walked into the health food store and stopped in surprise. Drew and Geena Bush were sitting at a table by the window drinking tea. As the Aldens walked toward the table, Drew got up. "Come up to the lodge for dinner sometime," he said. "When you find out what a great cook I am, you can tell all your clients and then they'll come to the lodge, too."

"I just wish I could convince you to sell it," said Geena. "But you're right. It's beautiful just the way it is."

Drew smiled slightly. "I have to admit, I don't always like it. It isn't the place I imagined ending up as a chef. But I'm beginning to like it."

They shook hands and the Aldens exchanged glances. Each knew what the other was thinking. Two suspects had just been eliminated from their list.

"Did you find any new clues?" Grandfather Alden asked them when they returned.

"Yes," said Henry. He, Benny, Violet, and Jessie filled their grandfather in on what had happened during their visit to Saranac Lake.

"Sounds like you are down to two suspects," said Grandfather Alden. "That's progress."

Henry nodded. But he was worried. How were they going to prove that Dr. Lin or Carl was behind the mystery of the lake monster?

The Aldens had just finished dinner and were about to start on dessert when Dr. Lin walked up to their table.

"How is the monster hunt going?" she asked.

"Ah, fine," said Jessie.

Dr. Lin smiled. "I hear you went into Saranac Lake to the library. It's a nice library. I did a little research on the possibility of a monster when I first arrived at Lake Lucille. But I reached the conclusion that Carl's stories were just that — stories."

Jessie was so surprised, she didn't know what to say. Without realizing it, Dr. Lin was eliminating herself as a suspect in the lake monster mystery.

"I wish there had been a monster," Dr. Lin went on. She shook her head regretfully. "Think of what a great discovery that would be!"

"Yes," agreed Henry, managing to speak at last. "You'd be famous."

Violet spoke up boldly. "Dr. Lin, where were you the night before last? When you said you were out camping and doing research?"

Without hesitation, Dr. Lin answered, "Near a place called Frozen Gap. I'm not exactly sure how to get there, but Carl could tell you. He's my guide on my overnight expeditions. I almost never go alone."

Once again the Aldens were struck speechless. They barely managed to say good-bye when Dr. Lin walked away.

"What's the matter?" Grandfather Alden asked, looking around at their unhappy faces.

"Oh, Grandfather," cried Jessie. "If Dr. Lin and Carl were out camping the night the monster footprints were made, then we don't have any suspects at all!"

"Is something wrong?" asked Nora just then, coming up to their table to refill their water glasses. "You've barely touched your desserts."

"Oh, no," said Violet quickly. She didn't want to hurt Nora's feelings — or Drew's. "It's delicious." She picked up her fork and took a bite of chocolate cake. She smiled. It really was good.

"I'm glad you like it," said Nora. She glanced across the room toward the table where the Duboises were sitting. "Someone was complaining tonight that we only had chocolate cake for dessert. But when I offered him ice cream, he said he didn't want that, either. I guess that shouldn't surprise me. He's been complaining ever since he got here." She shook her head. "Poor kid. He's as bad as Drew was when he first got here. He just wants to go back home."

Nora walked away.

Jessie said in a low, excited voice, "That's it!"

"What?" asked Benny.

"I think I know who's been making a monster appear at Lake Lucille. And I think I have an idea of how to catch the culprit!"

CHAPTER 9

A Monster-Maker

Later that night, the Aldens were setting up their trap on one of the paths by Lake Lucille.

"I'm tired of waiting," said Benny.

"Shhh," said Jessie.

"I hope Nicole is doing her job," said Henry. "Otherwise we won't catch anyone."

"I put a new roll of film into my camera," said Violet. "That way we can have *lots* of evidence." The Aldens had decided that the best way to catch a monster — a photograph — was the best way to catch their culprit, too.

Watch pricked up his ears and whined slightly. "Is that — " Benny began.

But a moment later, Nicole came down the path. "I think he fell for it," Nicole reported breathlessly. "I told him I had heard Nora and Drew talking and that Nora had said that if they had just one more monster incident, she was going to close the lodge for the summer — even if it's just more footprints on the beach. I said that she said, 'In fact, if I had seen those footprints, that would have been enough for me.' "

"That's great, Nicole," said Violet admiringly.

"I know," said Nicole. "And I pretended to be really upset."

"Excellent," said Jessie.

"Now, when he leaves tonight, follow him, but be careful not to get caught," Henry said.

"And don't forget your camera," Benny reminded her. "Just in case something goes wrong with Violet's."

Nicole nodded. "I won't," she said. "This time, we're going to have some solid proof of who the real monster of Lake Lucille is."

The night grew steadily darker. Stars appeared in the black sky. From far away, a bear hooted and a bear cub answered.

"Don't worry, Watch," Benny whispered. "They won't bother us if we don't bother them."

As the lights up at the lodge and in the cabins went out one by one, the whole world seemed to be going to sleep. Quiet and calm lay over the lake and the mountains.

Something rustled in the underbrush.

"What was that?" said Violet.

"Just an animal — a raccoon or opossum," Jessie whispered to her. "Carl told us they liked to go out at night."

"Oh, yes," said Violet.

"Shhh," said Henry very, very quietly.

Everyone froze in their hiding place. Benny put his hand over Watch's muzzle so Watch wouldn't bark.

Then a thin beam of light pricked the

darkness. It came down the trail. The Aldens could see that someone was walking, half covering the beam of the flashlight with one hand so that it wouldn't be as bright. Whoever it was wanted only enough light to see — and didn't want to be seen.

Turning on their flashlights, the Aldens leaped out from their hiding places and ran toward the light.

"Smile!" Violet said as she took a picture.

Jason Dubois was standing in the middle of the path, wearing an awful scowl. Nicole was right behind him.

He held up his hand to shield his eyes. "Nicole? Was this your idea? You're in big trouble!"

"I'm not in trouble. *You* are," Nicole answered.

Then for the first time, Jason realized that Nicole wasn't the only one on the path with him.

"Who — It's the Aldens," he said. "What are you doing here?"

"Catching a monster," said Benny.

"That's right," said Nicole.

By the beams of their flashlights, they saw the frightened look that suddenly crossed Jason's face. "W-What are you talking about?"

"You," said Henry. "You're the one who's been trying to make everyone think there is a monster around here."

"Don't be ridiculous," Jason said.

"If you're not the monster, why are you carrying a monster foot around with you in the middle of the night?" asked Jessie. She pointed to the ground next to Jason's feet. There was a pair of flippers, the sort of flippers that swimmers use when they go snorkeling. But these flippers were different. They had metal nails taped to the ends of them with silver electrical tape.

Jason said, "I don't know where those came from. I've never seen them before."

"Then why does one of the flippers have your name on it?" asked Violet.

"Uh . . ." said Jason. "Uh . . ."

"Admit it," said Henry. "You're the lake monster. You're Lucy."

Suddenly Jason's shoulders slumped.

"Okay, I am. At first I just did it for fun. I found an old air horn in the storage shed that was almost worn out. I wrapped a couple of towels around it and snuck out one night and used it to make sounds like I thought a lake monster would make. And you guys fell for it!

"That's when I got the idea of trying to make everybody believe there really was a monster. I thought if I could scare Mom and Dad, they'd take us home."

"That was rotten, Jason," said Nicole angrily. "When you fell out of the canoe, I thought you were really in trouble!"

"How did you do that?" asked Henry.

"I borrowed a jigsaw from the toolshed when no one was around and cut teeth marks in the paddle. Then I used it to paddle out onto the lake not too far from where you guys were having your picnic." Jason made a face. "I didn't count on Carl being around. I was afraid he'd catch on. That's why I was so rude to him."

"And the footprints — how did you leave

footprints on the beach without leaving any others?" asked Jessie.

"I knew that since it had been raining, the ground would be soft, so I waded all the way over to where I got out of the water. Then I put on the flippers and walked up on the beach to make the footprints. Afterward, I waded back," said Jason.

"That's why Watch went to the other end of the porch. He could smell you, or hear you, as you waded back," said Jessie.

"I guess," said Jason. "But tonight I didn't have to wade, because it hadn't been raining and so the ground was dry and firm. I didn't know that Nicole was making up everything about Nora being ready to leave."

"And you kept saying there was no monster so that no one would suspect you," said Violet.

"But we caught you!" cried Benny. "We tricked you and trapped you and you have the monster feet."

"Okay, okay," said Jason. "I did it. What are you going to do about it?"

"Either we tell Nora or you do," said Henry. "She and Drew are the ones who lost business because of what you did. You at least owe her an apology."

"I know," said Jason. Then he said, "I'm sorry. You know, I'm almost relieved it didn't work. Once I started going out in the canoe and walking around the lake and all that, I started kind of liking it here."

He pointed to Violet's camera. "How did you think of that?" he said.

"We did what you did," said Jessie. "We listened to Carl's stories. That's what gave us the idea of taking a picture. Carl's stories started the lake monster mystery — and they helped solve it, too."

CHAPTER 10

Who Loves Lucy?

"I don't want to leave tomorrow," said Benny. "Watch and I want to stay here forever."

"I wish we could stay, too, Benny," Grandfather Alden said. "But it's time to go home. We'll come back again, though."

"You are always welcome," Nora said. "In fact, I'm thinking of renaming Black Bear Cabin. I thought I might call it Lucy's Cabin."

The Aldens all laughed. So did the rest of the crowd assembled on the porch of the lodge after dinner. They were waiting for Drew to serve a special cake that he had made just for the occasion.

"Am I too late for cake?" a gruff voice asked from the darkness outside the screened porch.

"Not at all, Carl," Nora said. "Come on up."

Carl came up the stairs, pushed open the screen door, and walked onto the porch with Wildman at his heels. He pointed to a place by the door. "Wildman, stay," he said.

Wildman wagged his tail slightly, lay down, and put his head on his paws.

"We should have brought Watch to dinner," said Benny.

"That's okay, Benny. I think Drew made a special treat for Watch. And for Wildman, too," said Nora.

Just then the lights in the dining room behind them dimmed. They turned to see Drew and Jason walking toward them, holding between them a huge cake decorated with candles. They put the cake on the porch table and said, "Everybody blow out the candles for luck."

So everyone blew out the candles. Then Drew cut the cake and passed the pieces around.

"This is delicious, Drew," said Dr. Lin. "What do you call it?"

"It's the new specialty of the lodge," said Drew. "Monster cake!" Everyone laughed again — even Jason, who looked a little sheepish. Nora and Drew had forgiven him — and given him a job helping them with the lodge for the rest of the summer. He was already working in the kitchen, learning how to cook. He looked happier than the Aldens had seen him look since they'd arrived at Lake Lucille.

"I like it!" Benny declared.

Everyone agreed with him.

Nora came over to stand next to the Aldens. "Thank you for solving the lake monster mystery," she said softly.

"We didn't solve the whole mystery," said Jessie. "I still don't know who erased the footprints."

"Or who turned over Carl's canoe," added Violet.

Nora looked a little embarrassed. "I'm the one who erased the footprints," she said. "I was afraid there really might be a monster — and I didn't want any proof around."

"Oh!" said Violet.

A gruff voice said, "And I guess I never really had the monster turn me over in my canoe."

"You didn't?" Henry asked. "You made that up?"

"Well, I've turned over in my canoe before," said Carl. "But I made up the story because I was afraid the Parkers were gonna fancy up the lodge and have a lot of careless tourists who didn't care about the wilderness come up here trampling things and scaring the animals."

"But we weren't, Carl. You knew I wouldn't let that happen," Nora protested.

Carl nodded. "I realized it after a while. That's why it shook me up so much when I saw that paddle. I almost felt as if I'd made up a monster and then it had come to life."

Suddenly a long, low sound echoed across Lake Lucille.

Everyone stopped talking. Wildman raised his head.

"A bear," said Dr. Lin. "Right, Carl?"

The sound came again, more softly now, before it faded away.

Carl put down his cake plate in amazement. He stared out into the darkness. "It doesn't sound like any bear I've ever heard — or any other animal around these parts."

"No," said Dr. Lin softly. "It doesn't."

Benny bounced up from his seat. "It's Lucy," he said. "See? I *knew* she was real. It's Lucy and she's saying she's not a monster. She would never bite a paddle or turn over a canoe or hurt anybody."

"Maybe you're right, Benny," said Nora. "Maybe you are right after all."

Everyone laughed — everyone except Benny. He waved at the darkness in the direction of the lake. "It's okay, Lucy," he called. "See you next year!"

GERTRUDE CHANDLER WARNER discovered when she was teaching that many readers who like an exciting story could find no books that were both easy and fun to read. She decided to try to meet this need, and her first book, *The Boxcar Children*, quickly proved she had succeeded.

Miss Warner drew on her own experiences to write the mystery. As a child she spent hours watching trains go by on the tracks opposite her family home. She often dreamed about what it would be like to set up housekeeping in a caboose or freight car — the situation the Alden children find themselves in.

When Miss Warner received requests for more adventures involving Henry, Jessie, Violet, and Benny Alden, she began additional stories. In each, she chose a special setting and introduced unusual or eccentric characters who liked the unpredictable.

While the mystery element is central to each of Miss Warner's books, she never thought of them as strictly juvenile mysteries. She liked to stress the Aldens' independence and resoucefulness and their solid New England devotion to using up and making do. The Aldens go about most of their adventures with as little adult supervision as possible — something else that delights young readers.

Miss Warner lived in Putnam, Connecticut, until her death in 1979. During her lifetime, she received hundreds of letters from girls and boys telling her how much they liked her books.